Gemma's Open Doors provide fresh stories, new ideas, and essential resources for young people and adults as they embrace the power of reading and the written word.

Brian Bouldrey
Series Editor

GEMMA

Open Door

For Brian Bouldrey, who loves the trail
and the transformation.

PROLOGUE

Like all gifts from the gods, the bear suit first came to Rollo in dreams. One night in the middle of winter, he dreamed of finding a black bearskin on a trail in the woods. It lay across his path, and at first he thought it was a real bear asleep on the ground. As he came closer, he saw that it was an empty skin.

For some reason, he wasn't sure why, Rollo walked toward it. He picked the skin up and ran his hand over the dusty, rough brown fur. Then he turned it over and looked at the raw underside. It was yellowish and dry, with the texture of beef jerky. The hide was light as a leaf, long and flat as a plank, hollow as a husk. He sniffed it and found it smelled of old muscle and the ghost of blood. It was complete: the fangs in the mouth, the claws at the ends of the paws, the round, leathery pads at the bottoms of the feet. The eyes of the bearskin were shut tight. There was no telling what was behind the lids. The black nose was hard and shriveled as a prune.

Just add water, Rollo thought in his dream. *Just add water*, the spirit of the dried-out bear told him, speaking inside his mind.

ONE

April came. The snow was still deep in the passes of the Sierra Nevada mountains, but the foothills were covered in pale green grass. From the town where he lived down in the valley, Rollo could see the foothills on clear days. They seemed to float up from the valley floor. Behind them, like a film set, rose the high mountains with white snow capping the peaks. When Rollo looked at them he felt an ache in his heart. In his mind, he ran over his plans for escape.

Rollo endured the winter in town because he had no choice. Living there meant living in the messed-up, man-made world like everyone else. He hated every minute of it. At twenty-seven, he still lived in the converted garage at his mother's house and worked at a supermarket for money. He had no car, no girlfriend, and no friends, unless you counted people he knew from high school. He sometimes saw familiar faces in the mall. He rode his bike everywhere and took classes in environmental science at the junior college. School had nothing to teach Rollo. He knew everything about nature already, but taking the courses kept his mother quiet. More and more these days, she worried about his future.

He used to tell his mother that his future was in the mountains. But then she got the idea that Rollo planned to become a park ranger. For a while, this thought made her happy, and she went around telling her friends that Rollo "had his heart set" on joining the Forest Service. She liked the idea so much that she kept bringing it up, asking him what steps he had to take to join the service, what certifications he would need. When she offered to give him money to buy his first uniform, he finally told her the truth. Angrily, he shouted that he would never in a million years want to become a park ranger. He thought park rangers were just a kind of police force for nature. He would never, ever agree to be part of anything like that.

His mother started to cry when Rollo told her that what he really wanted was to become *part* of the park.

Rollo tacked up a row of maps on the walls of his room. He placed them so they lined up perfectly and made one big, continuous map of the length of the Sierra Nevada mountain range. The maps were very detailed, the best Rollo could find. They showed all the land-forms: rivers, forests, hills and valleys, lakes. They showed the steepness of the mountains using fine brown contour lines that swirled like fingerprints around the peaks. Where the lines were far apart, it meant the land rose gently. Where they were close together, it meant the grade was steep.

Rollo stood in front of the wall of maps for hours at a time. He traced routes with his index finger and imagined hiking along them. He chose the steepest paths, the ones that cut straight up the close-packed contour lines. He could almost sense how hard those hikes would be, and how he would feel when he reached the top of the mountain and stood there, alone. He laughed loudly to himself.

"Are you all right in there?" It was his mother, calling through his locked door. Her ears were as sensitive as a bat's.

Rollo didn't bother answering her. He felt trapped. He couldn't wait another minute to be away from here. To be in the mountains. He dragged his old green pack out from under his bed. For many seasons, that pack had been his only friend as he hiked through the wilderness. He opened the top and turned it upside down. A small pinecone and a handful of glittering mica dust fell onto his bed. He put his face inside the pack and breathed in the smell of woodsmoke and pine needles. It calmed him down. He stayed that way, with his head in the pack, until he heard his mother go away.

TWO

Rollo's idea of paradise was a wilderness without people. It was the Garden of Eden after the angel with the burning sword had thrown Adam and Eve out.

It wasn't that he hated other human beings on a personal level. He wasn't one of those crazy guys who showed up in public places with guns. He just didn't see the point to people. He wished they would painlessly disappear forever. They annoyed him with their silly questions and their demands. He wasn't interested in the things they made, like cars and computers and buildings. He had no use for the stupid gizmos, like cell phones, that they got so excited about. What good were cell phones when all you could do with them was talk to other human beings?

But although Rollo didn't really hate people, he did hate what they were doing to the planet. He thought about this all the time. It kept him awake at night. He followed the news about climate change and believed that human beings were causing it by burning too many fossil fuels. He knew that many animals were dying out because humans were destroying their habitats.

All this made Rollo angry, but it didn't surprise him one bit. It was exactly what he expected from mankind. Human beings were big fat hogs, in his opinion. There was no limit to how much of the earth they would take for themselves. They would leave nothing for plants or animals—or for people like him, who only wanted to be left alone.

Rollo could see the changes all around him. He watched his town grow and spread like a stain across the flat floor of the valley. Every year it got bigger. It ate up the fields where farmers once grew crops and littered the earth with cheap little houses and huge discount stores. At the same time, the air became more and more polluted because there were more and more cars. Rollo's town now had the worst air quality of any town in the whole United States! He had read that in a magazine, but he could have guessed it. When he rode his bike on days when the air was bad, his lungs burned like they were on fire.

Rollo knew he wasn't the only one

who thought about these problems. Some people marched in the streets about them. Some people signed petitions. Some people went to the state capital or to Washington, D.C., and held demonstrations. Rollo thought all that was a total waste of time. He would never join any group or sign any petition. Human beings would never stop being greedy and selfish, no matter what he did. His answer was to turn his back on the whole human mess and lose himself in the mountains.

The trouble was, he had never found a way to do it permanently. He wanted to arrange things so he didn't have to come back.

* * *

Dried noodles, powdered milk, granola: Rollo started making the list of food to take on his summer hiking trip.

Making this list always frustrated him. Food was Rollo's weakness. No matter how carefully he planned or packed, he could never carry enough to last him more than a few weeks. He ate very little and always lost a lot of weight during his trips. Sooner or later, though, the food always ran out.

When this happened, he'd live off nuts for a few days, eating them straight out of his greasy pockets. Sometimes he'd try eating plants and roots he found by the trail, but these always gave him a stomachache. Once he tried eating a caterpillar, but it tasted so bitter he had to spit it out. When he gave up on finding food in the wild, he'd go without eating for as long as possible. Five days was his record. But eventually, hunger and weakness would force him down into one of the tourist towns.

These towns lived off the summer vacation traffic to the mountains. After the silence of the high trails, they felt busy and noisy. They were full of revving motorcycles and giant, square white camper vans and whining, sunburned children. They made Rollo feel rattled. He walked through them with a scowl on his face, cursing the crowds of tourists, the fake log-cabin gift shops, the trash cans brimming with sticky paper plates. He'd grit his teeth and head straight for the local store, desperate to get his shopping over with and to escape back into the wild.

Usually, there was only one grocery in town, set up like an old-fashioned general store you'd see in a Western movie. These shops had a little bit of everything. They were the only places in town to buy food, so prices were sky-high. You could pay five dollars for a package of cheese, three for a box of crackers! This made Rollo mad. He sullenly gathered his food and paid in silence, only grunting when the cashier tried to talk to him.

Rollo felt defeated every time this happened. He had given in to his hungry, human side again and broken the magic spell of the mountains.

But that would never happen again, Rollo thought. He had dreamed of the bearskin, so it was all going to be different from now on. The dream had given him a brilliant idea.

THREE

The man at the costume rental company gave him funny looks when he went to rent the bear suit. He stared at Rollo, seeming to size him up. He asked him questions. He checked his ID.

"Is there a problem?" Rollo asked finally. "Do you have a bear costume I can rent or not? Should I go somewhere else?"

"No, no," the man said quickly. He was old and bald. His narrow shop was crammed with racks of colorful costumes. He turned and went into the back of the shop and returned with a furry brown shape on a hanger. The sight of it, empty and waiting, gave Rollo shivers.

The man said, "It's just that you don't strike me as the kind of person who'd go to a party dressed as a bear."

"What makes you say that?" Rollo asked, feeling offended.

The man shrugged and handed Rollo the costume.

Rollo tried it on in the curtained changing booth. It was heavy and made out of artificial dark brown hair. Like everything in the old man's shop, the bear suit had been used for many years. Its seams were worn, and it looked like some patches of fur had been gnawed by moths. There were places where the dark coating had rubbed off the claws, revealing the white plastic underneath. The costume had a strange smell that was like a mix of dry-cleaning chemicals, peanuts, and stale sweat. Rollo lowered the hollow bear head over his own and looked out through the bear's open mouth.

He studied his reflection in the mirror. His worst fear was that he'd look like a cute teddy bear in the suit. That would be embarrassing. But he thought he looked all right. "Raar," he said quietly, taking a swipe at the mirror with one paw.

"Excuse me?" asked the shopkeeper, from the other side of the curtain.

"I said, I'll take it," Rollo said. His voice echoed in the bear head and sounded loud in his own ears.

The last thing his mother said to him before he left for the mountains was,

"Whether you like it or not, son, I'm moving to the beach."

This surprised Rollo. When she came into his room in the garage, he expected her to ask when he was coming back from the mountains. Or to try to get him to change his mind and stay in town, the way she usually did. Instead, she told him she was moving.

"I'll leave my address with the neighbors," his mother said. "For when you come back." She wasn't crying when she said it. And she didn't sound angry, so Rollo knew she meant it.

This plan was news to Rollo. His mother loved the beach, and she had often talked about moving there. Maybe, now that he thought about it, she *had* been talking about moving to the beach a lot recently. But Rollo never listened. And he never imagined she would actually do it because he, Rollo, hated the beach. It was too far from the mountains, he told her. Too sandy, too flat, too wet.

Now his mother had made up her mind to go without him. Normally, this would have made Rollo angry. But with the bear suit hidden under his bed, he felt fine about it.

"That's okay," he said to his mother. "I'm not coming back this time."

She sighed. He could see she didn't believe him. She said, "All right, then. Whatever you say. But I'll leave my address, just in case."

FOUR

Rollo didn't know the girl who drove him into the mountains, and that was fine with him. He got in touch with her through a notice he'd put up on a bulletin board at the junior college. He gave her ten dollars for gas. That way he wasn't obliged to talk to her and her idiotic friends for the whole trip. He sat hunched in the backseat, clutching his pack on his knees while the rest of them talked and played bad rock music all the way to the mountains. It was a relief for them and for Rollo when they finally reached the Forest Service parking lot and he got out.

Without a word of thanks, he turned and started up the trail. In his pack he carried only a light tent, a sleeping bag, a stack of maps, a water bottle, a metal cup, and a small gas stove. And one more thing. Crushed in the darkness at the bottom of the pack was the bear suit, empty and waiting for him.

As he stretched his legs and the trail began to get steeper, his heart filled with joy. *Free*, he thought. *I am completely free.*

The first night, Rollo made camp in the forest, not far from an official park campground. He was excited and eager to try out his bear-suit plan. He was also hungry. He had decided not to bring any food on this trip. This way, he figured, he had to commit totally to his new way of living. It was hard to wait, but he decided not to put the bear suit on until after dark.

When night finally came, he went into his tent and got dressed. The body of the bear suit went on like hairy overalls, closing with a zipper at the front. The head went on like a helmet. Once it was in place, Rollo heard his own breathing echo in his ears like an obscene phone call. He crawled out of his tent on all fours. He tried the bear walk he had been practicing in his room for days: crouched down, knees bent, with his weight on his hands and his head swinging from side to side. It felt very different to do it outside, in the forest. It felt weird to be wearing a bear costume in the wilderness. Weird, but kind of good. Rollo decided he felt safe in the bear suit.

When the white moon came up over

the mountains, he shambled out and headed for the campground, still moving like a bear on all fours. By the time he reached his destination, sweat poured off him. His back and thighs ached from the effort of keeping up the bearlike walk. His head pounded from lack of oxygen because only a small amount of air came in through the bear head's open mouth. He felt dizzy.

Rollo sat down behind a patch of scrub and pulled the head off, gasping for breath. Just walking down the trail in the bear suit was harder than climbing a mountain! For the first time, he doubted his plan. Could this work? Was he strong enough? Only sheer stubbornness and the thought of having to go back down to the valley to buy food drove Rollo on.

The official Forest Service campground lay in a small valley below Rollo, not far away. By the light of the moon, he could see several tents scattered among the pine trees and wooden picnic tables. It was a low-altitude site. The campers who used it were weekend hikers, older people, Scout troops, and families who came to the mountains for a few days at a time. In other words, they were softies, not serious hikers like Rollo.

As he looked down, he half expected to see them all sitting around a fire, roasting marshmallows and singing cowboy songs. But everything in the camp was silent and still. Everyone seemed to be asleep.

Taking one last deep breath, he replaced the bear head and started down.

FIVE

Rollo's heart was beating fast as he entered the campsite. His instinct was to go cautiously and silently, but then he thought again. A bear wouldn't be quiet or timid, would he? A bear would be bold, casual, even noisy if he felt like it. A bear wouldn't worry about what the people in the camp thought about him, because he was a bear.

Moving on all fours, Rollo began to explore, looking for food. He sniffed and snuffled near the tents, hoping to find a bag of groceries left in the open. Nothing. He checked out the picnic tables, but they were clean. There was no trash lying around and nothing attractive to eat in the trash cans. Whoever these campers were, Rollo thought grumpily, they were tidy—too tidy. He had imagined they would be careless, ignoring the advice of the park rangers, and that he would find food easily. But no. The way things were going, he would have to break into the bear locker.

The bear locker was a big brown metal box sitting at the edge of the site. This was where campers were supposed to store all their food, to keep from attracting bears. Rollo had hoped to avoid taking food from bear lockers because it would make his raiding work almost too easy. It would be more like going to a convenience store than finding food in the wild. But by now his stomach was growling like a small animal. Morning was approaching, and he was in a hurry.

He stood upright to turn the handles that opened the locker. The paws of the bear suit made his hands clumsy, and it was hard for him to work the mechanism. It was difficult for him to see, too, because the bear head limited his field of vision. Rollo thought for one foolish moment of taking it off. It was a good thing he didn't, though, because just at that moment he heard voices.

"Did you hear that?" a boy's voice said in an excited whisper. The voice came from the nearest tent.

"I don't hear anything," a man answered sleepily. "Go back to bed."

"Listen. There's something out there." There was a pause. "I think it's a bear."

"It's not a bear, Zack. It's probably just a raccoon."

"It's way too big for a raccoon, Dad."

Now Rollo knew he had to be quick. Soon the whole camp would wake up and find him stealing their food. The angry hikers would surround him. They would strip the bear suit off and park rangers would come and haul him away to jail.

He yanked the door of the locker open. Its rusty hinges made a loud metallic squeak. He grabbed a bag of food and stuffed it under his arm. Then he turned, ready to run away. Immediately, he was caught in a bright beam of light. He froze in his tracks. Forgetting for a split second that he was supposed to be a bear, he almost held up his hands like an escaped prisoner.

"It *is* a bear!" the boy said. He

sounded delighted to see Rollo. The flashlight flicked back and forth across Rollo's face. "Hey, Dad! I told you it was a bear."

"Get back in here," said the second voice, wide-awake now. "You heard what the rangers said. Don't go near it. Leave it alone."

Rollo stood still, not knowing what to do. The beam from the flashlight stopped moving and came to rest on his body.

"Scabby, skinny-looking thing anyway," the boy said thoughtfully. "Not at all like in the pictures. It must be sick or something."

"Zack!" the voice in the tent commanded. "You get back in here this minute! It might have rabies."

"I don't think bears can get rabies," the boy said. Rollo heard him take a step closer. "Maybe he's just old."

Rollo came to his senses. Dropping the sack of food, he got down on all fours and charged toward the boy, growling and snarling for all he was worth. The child gave a little scream and dropped the flashlight as he dived into the tent and quickly zipped the door closed. Rollo stomped around the tent for a few minutes, snuffling and growling to make sure Zack and his dad stayed inside. Then he picked up the food bag and made his way back to his own camp.

By the time he arrived, it was near dawn. In the stolen food bag he found a box of cookies, a package of sliced ham, three hard green apples, some pale, rubbery cheese, and a chocolate bar. Almost too tired to eat, he wolfed down the cookies and left the rest for the morning. Then he peeled off the bear suit and jammed it into the bottom of his sleeping bag. He slipped in after it. With his toes he could feel its rough fur, the hard, hollow cask of the headpiece, the cold plastic of the nose.

Exhausted but wired, Rollo couldn't get to sleep right away. He watched the stars for a while. He wondered which group of them made up the Great Bear constellation.

He had never bothered to learn the constellations because they seemed to him like pointless human inventions.

Now he thought for the first time about how ancient they were, those imaginary line drawings in the sky. And he thought about the people who made them up. Back then, in the past, people lived with bears. They hunted them and feared them and loved them. They cooked up stories about them—weren't there a lot of old stories and fairy tales about bears? That was why they drew their shapes in the sky. It made sense to Rollo now.

People today wouldn't do that, he thought as he finally closed his eyes. They didn't think enough about bears. They would draw pictures of cars or computers or maybe superheroes across the stars instead. Those would be the boring modern constellations.

SIX

With the ripening of summer, Rollo moved higher into the mountains and deeper into his life as a bear.

He traveled north, following the length of the mountain range. He avoided the main trails and chose his own paths. This way, he enjoyed many beautiful days of hiking without meeting a single person. He was able to pretend, for hours at a time, that he was the only human being in the mountains. That was exactly how he liked it.

There was one small problem. Rollo couldn't let himself go too far from the busy trails. He needed the other hikers and the food they brought into the mountains. At night he'd make camp close to official campsites, but out of view. He didn't like being so near other people, but his raiding base had to be an easy bear walk from his dinner.

At night, Rollo put on the bear suit and went out to find food. He headed straight for the campsites, using the main trails and walking normally to save energy. Once he spotted the camp, he'd get down on all fours and start the bear act. He now made as much noise as possible at the beginning of a raid, snapping twigs, stomping through the bushes, even bumping up against tents with his whole weight. This scared the campers and made them stay inside. He'd learned his lesson after that first raid.

Getting the food was usually the least difficult part of the performance.

The metal bear lockers made it easy to locate. They were simple to open (for someone who wasn't a bear) and always full of whatever food Rollo was hungry for. The pickings were good. In the middle of summer, crowds of people trooped through the mountains. They brought fresh avocadoes, tortilla chips, jars of peanut butter, jelly, Coca-Cola, granola, fluffy white bread—everything! They put it all in the bear lockers, waiting for Rollo to come and take it. Once he even found an expensive sirloin steak and a bunch of asparagus. What were they thinking?

Rollo was eating better than he ever had on a hiking trip, better than he ate at home! On some days, when a raid had been particularly successful, he woke up feeling bloated and slightly hungover, like he'd been to a wild party.

Rollo felt a little ashamed when this happened. Hiking trips should be hard and hungry adventures, tests of strength. The famous wilderness pioneer John Muir, one of Rollo's heroes, used to walk these trails for months eating nothing but crackers! John Muir would disapprove of Rollo's indigestion.

Rollo had been eating the best food in the mountains for a few weeks now. He was putting on weight. All the late-night binging was making his shorts tight around the waist.

But the situation was temporary, he told himself. Once he hit the high country, everything would be different. Up there, there were no official campsites and no bear lockers full of rich food. The campers were different up there, too. They weren't soft city people dressed in brand-new wilderness clothing. They weren't the kind of people who brought *steak* to eat in the mountains. Instead, they were tough individuals, serious hikers like Rollo.

He looked forward to it. He also worried he wouldn't find enough to eat.

As it turned out, food was no problem at all in the high country. The bear suit worked as well there as it had in the low campgrounds.

Up here, the hikers used different systems to keep bears from eating their food. Sometimes they put the food in a bag and hung it from the branch of a tree. More often, they used bear canisters. These were plastic containers that were supposed to be bear-proof. Hikers put their food in them at night, then hid them at a distance from their campsites.

Neither of these strategies stopped Rollo, of course. He climbed trees and cut down food bags with his knife. Easy! He located bear canisters and opened them in seconds. No problem!

The food he found inside was different than the food from the bear lockers in the low campsites. Up here, people carried mostly dried food, like nuts and quick-cooking noodles. This was exactly the kind of simple food Rollo had carried when he was just a hiker, before he became a part-time bear.

When Rollo stole from the serious high-country hikers, he knew he was ruining their trips. Without food, they would soon have to go down to the terrible tourist towns in the valleys. This didn't change anything for Rollo. He was happy to take their very last can of tuna, their last nut or pack of beef jerky. He didn't feel bad about it at all. He felt like the other hikers should be smart, like him, and get themselves a bear suit.

SEVEN

Rollo ran into the old woman late one afternoon. He was high up in the mountains and far off the main trail. He had a store of stolen food and was looking for a quiet, hidden place to rest for a few days.

He climbed a cliff and went up a narrow valley between two peaks. The valley was cool, shady, and very hidden. It had a stream running through it. There were soft green ferns and aspen trees with white trunks growing along the riverbank. It was the last place Rollo would have expected to run into another person. But when he came to a clearing between the aspens, there was the old woman, reading a book in a patch of sun.

There was something strange about her. Rollo saw it immediately. She was wearing a big man's checked lumberjack shirt and a pair of tan shorts. Her legs, stretched out in front of her, were stick thin. They made Rollo think of skeleton legs. On her head she wore a kind of fat turban. It made her head look very large compared to her long, skinny neck.

"Hi there!" she said in a friendly way when she saw Rollo. Her voice sounded too loud to be coming out of such a thin body.

Rollo was very annoyed to find this old woman in his secret spot. He looked around and saw that she had set up a tiny blue tent. She had even strung a hammock between two trees. This woman wasn't going anywhere soon! He felt even more annoyed. He walked around her camp without saying a word.

"Have a nice day!" she called to him. "Thanks for stopping by!" He thought he heard her laughing. He decided to come back later and steal all her food. That is, if the skinny old woman had any.

The raid didn't go the way Rollo planned. Something was funny about that night. The moon was full, and it was bright as day. Everything in the forest seemed to be awake, and so was the old woman. She was waiting for Rollo when he came stomping into her camp.

"Hi again," she said. "I thought that was you." She didn't seem surprised or the least bit upset to see him in the bear suit. She acted almost like she was expecting him. "How about some tea?" she asked.

Rollo wasn't sure why he sat down with her, but he did. He took off the bear head and put it on the ground beside him. He watched the old woman make mint tea in the moonlight on a little stove without using a flashlight. Her wrists were so thin they looked as though a puff of wind could break them. They sat drinking the tea, listening to an owl hooting in a nearby tree. He could see the round shape of the old woman's funny turban, but not her face.

They didn't say anything for a long time. Rollo was used to people wanting to talk more than he did. But this woman's silence was making him nervous. Didn't she want to find out what he was doing in the bear suit? When she didn't say anything, Rollo began to realize he had questions to ask *her*.

"Have you come far on this trip?" he said finally. His voice was hoarse. He wasn't used to talking.

She shrugged. "Pretty far. Not as far as I usually like to go. My energy isn't what it used to be. But that's all right. I got myself here."

He thought she smiled at him in the darkness. He expected her to ask him a question now. That would be the normal thing for her to do. But she didn't say anything. Instead, she started humming. Rollo wondered if the old woman might be a little high on something.

"Are you all right?" he asked finally.

Now she threw back her head and

laughed loudly. Rollo heard the owl fly away through the trees, scared by the noise.

"I am really and truly not all right!" the old woman said. "I'm about as not all right as a person can be. But thank you for asking."

"I think you may be a little crazy," Rollo said to her.

She laughed again. "That's pretty funny coming from a guy wearing a bear costume in the forest." Who was this smart-alecky old lady?

Rollo felt offended. He got up to leave, but she stopped him. "I'm sorry," she said. "Please don't go yet. There's something I want to ask you."

Rollo said, "I'm not going to tell you about the bear suit."

"Not about that," the old woman said. "The bear suit is your business, if it is a bear suit."

"What do you mean by that?"

"Nothing," she said. "Ignore me. It's just the pills. They make me a little silly sometimes." She patted the ground next to her, and he sat down beside her again. She leaned against him and spoke in a quiet voice. "I know you know these mountains," she said. "Of course you do, they're your mountains. They belong to you. You've always lived here. So, advise me. What do I do now? How much farther do I need to go?"

"How much farther?" Rollo asked. "For what?"

"You know!" She elbowed him in the ribs. "To finish it. To go all the way. I mean, I thought this place was ideal. I thought no one would ever find me here. But then you show up and I see that it's not safe. Oh, I'm not upset at you, just the opposite! I'm glad it was you and no one else. But I don't want the others coming around, at least not for a few more days. After that—" she took a deep breath and let it out. "It will be fine."

Rollo wasn't sure why the old lady was saying these things, but now he was certain that she was both crazy and high. Still, she was interesting. And she felt the way he did about people. He decided to help her. He thought for a few moments about her problem.

"Just stay here," he said after a pause. "Regular people don't ever come up here. No one else is going to find you."

"Well, that's a relief!" the old woman said. She stood up with difficulty. For the first time, Rollo realized that she was very weak and in pain. "Thank you," she said. "Whoever you are. Thank you for coming to help me. Will I see you tomorrow?"

"No," Rollo said. He had already stayed too long and said too much. "You won't see me again."

"And you never saw me at all," the old woman said, touching her finger to the side of her nose. "Remember that."

EIGHT

The days began to blend together. Rollo could go for weeks without seeing another person. One evening when it was still light, a bear wandered into Rollo's camp.

Rollo was resting in his tent, dressed in the bear suit and waiting to go out on a raid. He heard the bear before he saw it. It came sniffing and grunting and padding around the tent. He put on the bear head, poked it out of the flap, and called to the bear.

"Hey!" he yelled. "Hey you!"

The bear was nosing around his backpack, trying to lift it with one paw. When it heard Rollo, it raised its head and looked straight at him. It was a small bear with dark, almost black, fur. Its face was pale brown, the color of milky coffee. Its eyes were small and shiny. It looked young. When it saw Rollo, it lifted its upper lip and growled, not very seriously. Then it went back to examining his pack.

"Hey, hey!" Rollo said. "I'm talking to you." He stepped out of the tent and stood in front of the bear with his hands on his hips. He felt no fear. "What exactly do you think you're doing?"

The bear looked at him again. It seemed surprised to see a man dressed like a bear, but only a little. It stared at Rollo with a confused expression and growled again. It took a step backward.

"You'd better move along," Rollo warned the bear. "This is my territory."

A crazy idea suddenly came to him. It crossed his mind that this was not a real bear at all, but another impostor like himself. He half expected the bear to stand up, take off his head, and start telling Rollo about his own adventures pretending to be a bear. This thought struck Rollo as funny, and he began to giggle. Once he started laughing, something took hold of him and he found he couldn't stop.

"You're a copycat," he said to the bear. "It was my idea first. And you're doing a really bad job of being a bear! I mean, look at that fur! It's much too shiny. Look at your paws! Do you wash them with soap and water? Do you use hand cream? You don't even move like a bear, you loser. Look, you've got to use your back legs, really put your rear end into it."

Rollo dropped down and started to show the bear what he meant. But the bear was already gone, running away through the trees as fast as it could go.

NINE

Early one morning, Rollo woke to find a white mule pushing its nose through his tent flap. On its back was a female park ranger in a broad-brimmed green hat and a brown cotton uniform.

I am caught, thought Rollo when he saw her. *The nature police have found me*.

He crawled out of his tent, suddenly wide-awake and very nervous. The bear suit lay where he had dumped it, in a pile just inside the tent. It was a good thing Rollo had taken it off the night before. He often didn't bother these days. He prayed the wind wouldn't blow the tent flap open so the ranger could see it.

"Morning," she said, politely touching her fingers to the brim of her hat. She got off her mule and, in a gesture that was strange because they were standing on a mountaintop, she held out a hand for Rollo to shake. Rollo saw that his own hands were filthy. He wiped one on his t-shirt, which was just as dirty, and held it out to the ranger.

"I wondered if you could help us," she said. She had rosy, tanned cheeks and wore her blond hair in a long braid down her back. A silver badge pinned on her shirt said her name was Ranger Quinn. "We're getting some reports of increased bear activity in this area. Have you had any problems?"

Rollo scratched his shaggy head and tried to look like he was thinking. Inside, he was panicking. How much did this ranger know? Was she playing games with him, trying to trap him?

"I haven't had any trouble with bears," he said.

"No little visits in the night? No food stolen?"

He moved his hand from his head and started scratching his beard. It had grown long. He found a leaf in it and picked it out. "Nope," he told Quinn. "Nothing."

"Are you sure about that?" Quinn looked around Rollo's campsite with raised eyebrows.

The night before, Rollo had stolen food from a church youth group that was camping beside a nearby lake. It was a big, happy group of parents and children, and they had brought a lot of delicious homemade food with them. They stayed up late, singing songs around the campfire while Rollo, who was watching from the woods, got hungrier and more impatient. When the campers finally went to bed, Rollo stomped into their camp and took all the food he could find—probably more than he needed. When he got back to his own camp, he had stuffed himself with hot dogs and potato salad and beer. Then he fell asleep, leaving his dirty dishes, uneaten food, and garbage lying around on the ground. His campsite looked like a hurricane had hit it. No—it looked like a bear had raided it.

Ranger Quinn's rosy face seemed to cloud over as she gazed at the mess. A suspicious expression came into her eyes. "Do you have a bear canister with you?" she asked, sounding official. "Can you show it to me?"

Fortunately, Rollo had stolen a bear canister a few days before. He brought it out and showed it to Ranger Quinn. The canister looked like a little barrel made of thick black plastic. It was big enough to hold a small amount of food, enough for just a few days of hiking. It had a clever lid that locked with two screws.

Rollo hadn't intended to steal the canister. He'd found it when he was raiding a camp. He had opened many bear canisters before with no trouble. But, for some reason, he couldn't find a way to open this one in the dark. He'd had to carry the whole thing back with him to his own camp. Even then, it took him an hour to figure out how to get the lid off.

Quinn was glad to see the canister, but she scolded him. "You need to use this! If you leave food lying around your camp, I promise you will have a visit from a bear," she said.

And then, to Rollo's relief, she changed the subject.

"One more thing." Ranger Quinn reached into her back pocket and brought out a photograph. "Have you seen this woman on the trail?"

The woman in the photograph had on a white lab coat. Her gray hair was long and curly, and she wore a pair of glasses with red frames. The face was plumper than Rollo remembered, and she wore no turban, but he recognized the old woman immediately.

"I haven't seen her," Rollo lied. "Who is she? What did she do?"

Quinn shook her head sadly and put the picture back in her pocket. "Oh, she didn't do anything," Quinn said. "At least not in my opinion. She's Doctor Elaine Minter-Moore, a cardiologist. But her family is looking for her. They think she may have come up here because—well, because this is one of her favorite places in the whole world." Quinn waved her hand at the scene around them. "I can't say I blame her, can you?"

Rollo had set up his camp in a meadow near the top of a high mountain. The site was surrounded on four sides by dark green pine trees that filled the air with a warm, spicy scent. The meadow grass was bright green, and little wildflowers, red and yellow and white, grew up through it. A stream of cold, clean water flowed over smooth stones through the middle of the meadow. It made a small waterfall as it fell over some boulders. At the bottom, there was a deep pool for swimming, surrounded by flat, sunbaked slabs of rock for drying off.

Rollo thought of that other campsite. That cool, shady one in the hidden valley where the old woman waited under the aspens. Maybe she was in the tent. Maybe she was in the hammock. He knew they would never find her, or at least not for a very long time. He was glad.

When Rollo looked at Quinn again, he saw a tear shining in her eye, an eye that was almost as blue as the sky. For an awful moment, he wondered if she might start to sing. For another awful moment, he wanted to tell her about the old lady, to let Quinn know that she was all right.

But he didn't say anything. Ranger Quinn only told him to clean up his garbage, use the bear canister, and look out for rattlesnakes when he sat on the flat rocks by the pool.

TEN

Quinn's visit sent Rollo even higher into the mountains. He walked along the spine of the range, above the tree line. There, the peaks were pure granite and as sharp as knife blades. Their steep slopes were covered with fields of broken gray rocks. The trails ran sideways across the jagged land like thin white threads. Even this late in the year, patches of snow still waited in the shadows of the valleys.

Up here, Rollo found the hard people. These were the men and women who, like Rollo, loved the farthest corners of the wilderness. He often spotted them at a distance. They would appear as a single black dot moving across the rocky slope, far away. They walked fast, like Rollo. Like Rollo, they were usually alone. When they passed him on the trail, they would nod, but never stop to talk.

Rollo might have made friends with some of these serious hikers. If they had stopped to talk, to eat a stolen meal together, they might have found they had things in common. Rollo had never been any good at making friends. Mostly he didn't need them. But sometimes in the past he'd thought it would be nice to find one or maybe two other people who saw the world the way he saw it.

Now, to be honest, he didn't see the point. He had gone too far. During the last few weeks of living as a part-time bear, he had crossed some line. Now he could hardly even tell one person from another. Men, women, old, young, serious, not serious—they all looked basically alike to him. They all looked like sources of dinner. At night, he raided their camps in the same way, for the same reason. An animal's hunger has no human loyalty, he told himself. Why should it?

The summer began to fade. The days grew shorter, and Rollo felt the autumn coming fast. The birds and animals were restless and busy preparing for the winter. The wind suddenly blew cold.

Rollo began wearing the bear suit during the day, for warmth. There were few other hikers on the trail now, so he didn't worry about being spotted. The suit was worse for the wear after a summer of constant use. It had lost a claw or two. Rollo had to sew patches on the knees. It stank, too, with a combination of woodsmoke, trail dust, stale food, and Rollo's own sweat. To Rollo, this was a comforting, familiar smell, like the smell of his own room. He altered the bear suit, making a flap under the tail so he could go to the toilet without taking it off. As he was doing this, he realized he would never be able to return it to the costume shop. But that was all right with him. He couldn't have given up the bear suit now.

One morning Rollo woke up to snow. His tent made a tunnel covered in soft powder. Rollo crawled out into a silent, white world. Nothing moved, not even the smallest bird. He was not cold as he shuffled around his camp in the bear suit, smelling the new smells of winter. But he knew what the snow meant. It meant he had to go down from the mountains. He had to take off the bear suit and return to the valley. He had to become Rollo again.

The thought practically broke his heart. It had been a beautiful, wild summer. Rollo had never been so free, or so well fed! He patted his belly, which bulged out under the matted fur of the bear suit. He studied his ragged paws. He pressed them together and looked up at the sky. *Just one more night*, he prayed.

Please, just one more.

ELEVEN

Rollo knew he had to go lower. There were no hikers left in the high country this late in the season. Winter was too close. The wind was too cold. He left his tent where it was, with his backpack inside. He didn't think he'd need those things now. Taking nothing with him, he started down the trail.

He wore the full bear suit, head and all. The slope was steep, the trail zig-zagged down, and his feet slid on the new snow. He walked for most of the day, but he didn't feel tired. He had no map, but he didn't need one. He knew the way by smell.

He reached the campsite by sunset. It was one of the official ones, low down and near the entrance to the park. It was still open. There were a few tents scattered around in the trees with a handful of tough campers staying in them. The bear locker stood, brown and square, on one side.

When Rollo saw the bear locker, he realized that this was the very first camp he had ever raided. He was back where he started. The thought made him smile. It seemed right.

He hid in the forest above the campsite and planned the raid—or he tried to. In the early days, Rollo had been smart about his raids. He put a lot of thought into them. He studied the target and planned his attack carefully. This was why he had never been caught.

Now when he looked down at the

campsite and tried to plan, Rollo felt his brain wasn't working correctly. Lately, this had been happening more and more. He was wide-awake. He felt fine, not sick or dizzy or scared. But when he tried to think ahead, into the future, his brain refused to cooperate. It was like it had lost the ability to think about anything but the present. His brain just didn't want to go any further than that.

After a while, he gave up trying. He shrugged his shoulders and settled down behind a big rock to wait. He didn't need to plan, he thought. He knew what to do.

He was right. He knew exactly what to do. He came out of the forest when the moon rose above the tops of the trees. He stomped and snuffled into the campsite. He spent some time exploring the picnic tables. He poked around the tents and heard the scared whispers of the campers inside. He was the perfect bear.

Then he went to the bear locker. It was harder to open than he remembered. He struggled with the lock, banged his paws against the door, and bellowed. Finally, the door broke and he was very happy. Inside he found breakfast cereal, bacon, and a bag of pears. Rollo loved pears. He hadn't found a single one all summer. He began eating them right away.

The pears were delicious, sweet and ripe. The juice slid down his chin. He sat by the locker and ate the whole bag, enjoying every bite.

It was all going fine for Rollo, until they shot him.

He heard the noise before he actually felt the impact. Lights suddenly came on all around him. People started shouting.

"Well, hello Fatso," a woman's voice said. Rollo thought it sounded like Ranger Quinn. "We've been looking everywhere for you."

He dropped the empty bag and stood up. He turned toward the lights and lifted his paws in the air. The glare blinded him. He could hear his attackers, but he couldn't see them.

"Will you look at the belly on him!" a man's voice said. "Someone's had a great summer." Several other people laughed. There seemed to be eight or ten of them standing around Rollo. Where had all these people come from? Had they been hiding in the tents?

Rollo opened his mouth to complain. *You people are very rude*, he wanted to say. *You're treating me like a clown. And your insults are too personal!* But before he could speak, Ranger Quinn gave the signal.

"Let's do it," she said in a firm voice. There was a loud pop.

That's when Rollo felt the first shot. Something sharp hit his right thigh. Now he knew these people were maniacs! He reached down to touch the wound and found a kind of dart sticking into his skin. He tried to shout for help, but no words came out, only roars. He took a step forward to ask for mercy. That's when they shot him again. This time the pain was in his neck. He fell to the ground.

"There he goes," Ranger Quinn said. Someone approached. Someone touched his head. "He's out cold."

TWELVE

When Rollo woke, he was lying on a mountainside in a field of snow. He sat up and looked around. He didn't recognize the place. It was in the highest part of the mountains, far, far from everything. There was nothing but snow and pine trees as far as he could see.

He studied the ground around him. Human feet had trampled the snow. A thin pair of tire tracks led away from him, across the mountainside. Ranger Quinn hadn't killed him. She and her criminal friends had driven Rollo up here and dumped him. But why?

Why? Rollo knew he should try to figure this out. A small, intelligent part of his brain knew he needed to get out of there fast. He knew the smart thing to do was to follow the tire tracks and get down to the valley as quickly as possible. Winter was here. He would not survive it on the mountain. The cold would kill him. Ranger Quinn must know that.

But most of Rollo's brain didn't care about the danger. All *it* wanted was to go to sleep. The two parts of his brain fought for a few seconds in his skull. The sleepy part won.

Instead of going down lower, Rollo climbed up until he found a little cave in the rocks. He used the last of his energy to clear a space inside. He crawled into it. There he curled up, tucking his nose under his paw. It was comfortable in the cave. He liked it here. He didn't feel afraid. The old woman was right. This was a good place to die.

And wasn't this what Rollo had always wanted? Wasn't that the whole reason for the bear suit? Now he would never have to live in the stupid, ugly, noisy human world again. He would never have to leave the wilderness. He would stay here forever. His bones would be part of the mountains.

Rollo didn't die: he dreamed. In his dream, he was walking along a trail in the forest. After a while he came to a place in a valley where there was a huge patch of blackberry bushes. The bushes were higher than his head, and they were covered in perfect, ripe blackberries. Rollo got very excited. He went up and began using his claws to pick the berries and shove them into his mouth. He did this for a long time. There were so many wonderful berries! Then he noticed that there were two other people nearby, both picking berries like him.

He recognized one of them right away. It was the old woman, Elaine—was that right? She was standing in the berry patch, pulling fruit from the bushes and eating it. Her mouth was stained with purple juice. She had a happy expression on her face and she looked very healthy. She had curly gray hair now, like in her picture. It was streaked with purple. Rollo saw that the berries were making her well.

The old woman raised a hand and waved to Rollo in a friendly way. "It's a great year for blackberries! We need to eat all we can," she said. The palm of her hand was dyed purple.

Rollo was glad to see the old woman again, and he was glad she had found this magical berry patch. There was more than enough for everyone. He didn't mind sharing with her at all.

The other person was farther away. Rollo didn't recognize him at first. He had long, dirty hair and a beard. He had a fat belly and wore nothing but a pair of filthy shorts and hiking boots. He stood in the middle of the berry patch, stuffing fruit into his mouth. Not only his lips, but his whole body was smeared with berry juice. He ate fast, gobbling and grabbing more berries. He made loud slurping noises. It was disgusting to watch him.

"Who is that?" Rollo asked the old woman.

"Don't you know?" she said. "I think you know."

"He'll eat all the berries," Rollo said. He felt worried and angry. He didn't like the look of this person at all. He stood up on his hind legs and roared. The dirty man looked up at him with small, mean, greedy eyes. Then Rollo chased him. He chased him and chased him for a long time until the man fell off a cliff and disappeared.

Rollo woke up. He dragged himself out of the cave and into the sunshine. There were still patches of snow on the mountainside, but most of it had melted. The ground was wet and muddy. Rollo sat down on a dry rock. He licked one paw clean, then the other. Then he used his clean paws to rub his face and ears. Finally he scratched himself all over, front and back, with his long claws. It felt good.

Rollo looked around. The world was brand-new with spring. He was alone in the deep wilderness, farther away from human life than he had ever been. The thought didn't scare him, but it didn't make him happy, either. Not now. He accepted it. It was normal, the way things were supposed to be.

Only one thing was bothering Rollo: he was starving. He was hungrier than he had ever been in his life. It was a good kind of hunger—he felt strong and well, not weak or sick. But he had to get food right away.

He wandered into the forest, turning over rotten logs and eating the insects and grubs he found underneath. He dug for roots and ate them. But he was still very, very hungry. He sniffed the wind again and again. What was he searching for? What did he want?

He didn't know the answer. But eventually he found what he was looking for, and then he remembered. It was human food. The smells of bacon, pancakes, and baked beans tickled his nose. The scent was faint. It came from very far away, but as soon as he smelled it, Rollo knew what he had to do. He pointed his nose downhill and started to walk, following the magical smells. He was heading for the trails that brought people into the mountains, bringing with them their wonderful, life-giving food.

VOCABULARY LIST

Bear canister: A small, portable container for food with a locking lid, used by hikers to protect food from bears.

Bear locker: A metal box for locking up food at a campground. Also called a bear-proof food locker.

Campground: An official camping place, often with facilities like toilets, water, and electricity.

Campsite: A small camping place, often in the wild, with few or no facilities.

Cardiologist: A doctor specializing in the heart.

Contour lines: Fine lines on a map that follow points of the same height and show the shape and steepness of the land.

Forest Service: An official U.S. agency that manages wilderness areas.

Great Bear constellation: A group of stars that can be seen in the night sky during most of the year in the Northern Hemisphere. It is one of the largest and best-known constellations.

John Muir (1838–1914): An important American author and naturalist who lived in California and wrote about its wild places. He was an early leader in nature conservation and has been called "the father of our national parks."

Park ranger: An official who works in a national park, nature reserve, or wilderness area, and who is responsible for the use and protection of the park.

Raid: A quick, surprise attack.

Sierra Nevada mountains: The large range of mountains on the West Coast of the United States. It runs 400 miles (640 kilometers) from north to south, mostly through the state of California.

Wilderness: A place that is natural, with no cities, towns, or farms; usually with few human inhabitants.

Marta Maretich

THE BEAR SUIT

In a varied career, Marta Maretich has been a teacher, a publisher, a journalist, an editor, and a fiction writer. She is the author of three novels: *The Merchants of Light* (2015), *The Possibility of Lions* (2011), and *The Bear Suit* (2017). Her short fiction, nonfiction, and poetry have appeared in many publications and been anthologized in collections including *Inspired Journeys: Travel Writers in Search of the Muse* (2016). She has been awarded artist residencies at the Eastern Frontiers Educational Foundation at Norton Island and Yaddo. Born in Nigeria and raised in California, Marta has lived in London since 1995.

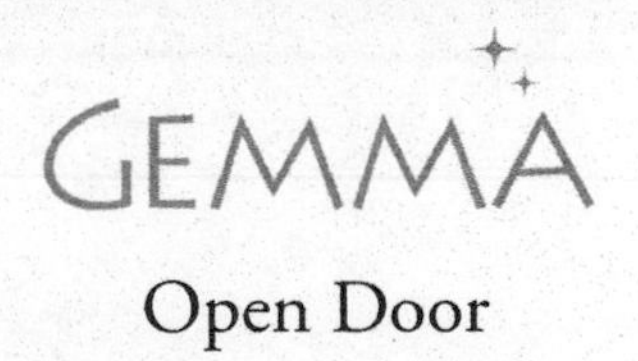

Open Door

First published by Gemma Open Door for Literacy in 2017.

Gemma Open Door for Literacy, Inc.
230 Commercial Street
Boston MA 02109 USA

www.gemmamedia.com

Printed in the United States of America

978-1-936846-55-9

Library of Congress Cataloging-in-Publication Data applied for

Cover by Laura Shaw Design